Eventually Mandy stopped in front of a cage. "This is Petal," she said with a smile. Gemma peered into the cage and gasped out loud. With her glossy brown coat, shiny wet black nose and huge chocolate eyes, she was absolutely adorable! Petal bounced over to the cage door and jumped up at the wire, her tail wagging like mad. *"Woof!"* she barked, as if she was saying "Hello".

Have you read all these books in the **Battersea Dogs & Cats Home** series?

BATTERSEA DOGS & CATS HOME

PETAL'S
story

by

Sarah Hawkins

Illustrated by Sharon Rentta
Puzzle illustrations by Jason Chapman

RED FOX

BATTERSEA DOGS & CATS HOME: PETAL'S STORY
A RED FOX BOOK 978 1 849 41580 4

First published in Great Britain by Red Fox,
an imprint of Random House Children's Publishers UK
A Random House Group Company

This edition published 2011

1 3 5 7 9 10 8 6 4 2

The Random House Group Limited supports the Forest Stewardship Council
(FSC®), the leading international forest certification organization. Our books
carrying the FSC label are printed on FSC®-certified paper. FSC is the only
forest certification scheme endorsed by the leading environmental
organizations, including Greenpeace. Our paper procurement policy can be
found at www.randomhouse.co.uk/environment.

MIX
Paper from
responsible sources
FSC® C016897

Set in 13/20 Stone Informal

Red Fox Books are published by Random House Children's Publishers UK,
61–63 Uxbridge Road, London W5 5SA

www.kidsatrandomhouse.co.uk
www.totallyrandombooks.co.uk

Addresses for companies within The Random House Group Limited
can be found at: www.randomhouse.co.uk/offices.htm

THE RANDOM HOUSE GROUP Limited Reg. No. 954009

A CIP catalogue record for this book is available from the British Library.

Printed and bound by CPI Group (UK) Ltd, Croydon, CR0 4YY

**Turn to page 91 for lots
of information on
Battersea Dogs & Cats Home,
plus some cool activities!**

🐾 🐾 🐾 🐾

Meet the stars of the Battersea Dogs & Cats Home series to date . . .

Bailey

Chester

Misty

Max

Rusty

Daisy

Snowy

Huey

Stella

Angel

Cosmo

Alfie

Buddy and Holly

Coco

Petal

An Important Letter

"Mum!" Gemma yelled, dropping her schoolbag at the bottom of the stairs. She tried to hang her coat on the rack, but there were so many others already there that it just sent a whole load of them sliding onto the floor. Gemma sighed and picked them up. Then she set off to find her mum.

There were noises coming from nearly

every room. Gemma
poked her head round
the door to the den.
Twelve-year-old
Alison was practising
the piano, and Pete
and Matthew, the ten-
year-old twins, were

fighting over the PlayStation controller.
The room was full of the sounds of
plonkety music and computer-game
explosions.

Gemma wandered into the kitchen,
where sixteen-year-old Hermione
was talking on the phone.
"What?" she
snapped at
Gemma when
she tried to ask
where Mum was.

"Nothing," Gemma mumbled, and
went to look upstairs. It wasn't easy
having six older brothers and sisters. No
one ever listened to her!

As Gemma went along the hallway
she saw that Lorna's bedroom door was
open. Inside, Lorna was packing things
into her suitcase. She patted her bed, and
Gemma went in to perch on it. She
fiddled with the bright bangles and shoes
Lorna was taking with her. Lorna wasn't
going on holiday – she was
eighteen, ten years older
than Gemma, and she
was leaving home and
going to university.

"What's up,
Gem?" Lorna
asked, pulling her
in for a hug.

"I wanted to tell Mum about this dog I saw on the way home," Gemma told her. "It was a Pekingese, and it was so cute! My friends said it was ugly, but I think it was adorable. Its nose was all squashed like this . . ."

Lorna giggled as Gemma pulled a face. "You are obsessed with dogs!" she laughed.

"Will you get a pet when you go to uni?" Gemma asked, looking at the suitcase.

"I don't think I'd be allowed," Lorna said. "Besides, I'm going to be much too busy studying."

"The first thing I'm going to do when I grow up is get a puppy of my own!"

Gemma declared. "I just wish I could grow up faster so I wouldn't have to wait so long."

Lorna looked at her seriously. "You know, you could ask Mum and Dad again about getting a dog. Alex will go back to uni in a few weeks, when the summer holidays are over, and now I'm going as well, there'll be a bit more space around here. You could tell Mum you're *so* upset I'm leaving that only a puppy can make it better!" Lorna put her hand on her forehead and flopped on the bed like a fainting lady.

"I *am* sad that you're not going to be here any more," Gemma sighed, looking out of the window over the back garden. She'd spent lots of time in here with Lorna. Now her sister Hermione was going to take Lorna's old room she'd probably never be allowed in here again!

"I'll be home to visit lots, Squirt, I promise. And if you get a puppy I'll have to come home and visit it too, won't I? Why don't you write Mum a letter listing all the reasons you should be allowed a dog? I'll help you."

"OK!" Gemma grinned. She could think of millions of reasons why she'd be the best dog owner ever!

Good News

Gemma and Lorna had a fun afternoon
thinking of every reason they could why
Gemma should be allowed a dog. At
dinner that night Lorna offered to take
everyone to the park the next day. "If we
leave Mum and Dad to have a peaceful
Saturday afternoon they'll be so happy
they'll agree to anything!" She winked at
Gemma.

Gemma went to bed fizzing with excitement, and stayed awake long after Alison had started snoring in the bed next to her. She crossed her fingers, her toes and even her eyes. *Please let Mum and Dad say yes*, she thought as hard as she could.

The next morning Gemma rushed around trying to convince everyone to come out with her and Lorna. She gathered up Pete and Matthew's bats and balls, helped Alex find his old Frisbee, and even raided her piggy bank to find enough money to promise Hermione and Alison an ice cream if they came too.

Eventually they were all
ready to go, but before
they left, Gemma
slipped her letter into
Mum's book. Mum
was a real
bookworm, and
spent every spare
second she had reading,
so Gemma knew she'd see it there.

They spent the afternoon playing
rounders and racing round the park.
"This would be a brilliant place to bring
a puppy," Gemma said to Lorna as they
sat on the grass.

"I'm exhausted!" Alison sighed as she
and the others ran up and flopped down
next to them. "The boys keep cheating
and hitting the ball as far as they can to
make me run!"

"Do not!" Pete protested.

"Let's do something less energetic for a minute," Lorna suggested. "How about charades?"

"That game we play at Christmas?" Matthew asked.

"I'll go first," Gemma said.

"Gemma's got an idea!" Lorna shouted over the others. "Gemma first."

Gemma stood in front of them all and began to act out her phrase.

"Film!" Alison guessed.

"Last word . . ." Gemma pointed at herself in the chest.

"Me!" Alex smiled.

Hermione sighed. *"Marley and Me,"* she guessed. "Of course. Can't you think about anything except dogs?"

"It's a good film!" Gemma protested. "And dogs are brilliant!" she yelled, chasing her big sister towards the duck pond.

"Aaarrggghhh!" Hermione squealed as she ran.

*

Gemma was starving by the time they got home. Pete and Matthew must have been too, because they ran in the front door straight into the kitchen.

"Don't go in the fridge!" Mum yelled as the twins came in. "Dinner's ready."

"Whooooo!" the boys cheered.

Gemma sank gratefully into a seat at the big table. Soon everyone was sitting down while Mum passed round their plates. Pete and Matthew were battling with their forks, Alison was reading a book and Hermione was texting on her phone, while Alex and Lorna talked about uni.

"Right everyone," Mum said as she put the last plate on the table and sat down next to Dad. "Shhhh, shhhh."

Gemma's breath caught in her throat as her mum started talking. Had she seen the letter yet? Was she going to say something about getting a puppy?

"I got a very interesting letter today . . ." Mum began, looking at Gemma with a straight face. Gemma couldn't tell if she was cross or not. Lorna squeezed her hand reassuringly. "It was from Gemma." Eight faces turned towards her, and Gemma's cheeks started to feel hot.

"It's not easy being the youngest in such a big family, you know," Mum went on, "always being shouted over and having to wear hand-me-down clothes."

"I have to wear Lorna's old clothes," Hermione pouted.

"Yes, but they've only been worn by one other person then, darling," Mum smiled. "By the time they get to poor old Gemma they're not *second*-hand, they're *fourth*-hand! I don't think Gemma's ever had anything new, something of her very own. And in her letter she told Daddy and I about the one thing that she really, really wants."

Gemma couldn't believe her ears.

"Can you guess what Gemma wants more than anything in the whole wide world?" Mum asked. Even Hermione was interested now; she'd put her phone down and was listening intently.

"A puppy." Gemma's voice was just a squeak, but this time her whole family heard her.

Mum looked at Gemma and burst out laughing. "Yes, a puppy! And since you want one so very, very much, and gave us such a lovely long list why you should be allowed one, Dad and I have decided we agree." She paused. Gemma stared at her mum in disbelief.

"You mean . . ." Gemma gasped. Mum nodded and jumped up to give Gemma a hug.

"We're getting you a puppy of your very own!"

Soon everyone in her family was crowding round Gemma's chair in a noisy happy hug. "You're getting a puppy, Gem," Lorna cheered. "We did it!"

"Can't we have a dog too?" Pete asked, looking at Matthew.

"I think one puppy in the family is enough," Dad replied. "The house is pretty crowded as it is, without us each having a dog! We can all help out with Gemma's dog, but he'll mainly be hers."

"That is so unfair," Hermione moaned.

"It's cool!" Alison smiled. "Can I take it on walks, Gemma?"

Gemma smiled at her sister, but she could only nod her head.

She didn't want to say anything to break
the magic. This was the most amazing
thing that had ever happened to her!
She'd wanted a puppy for so long – she
couldn't believe she was actually going to
get one. It felt like a wonderful dream.
And if it was a dream then she never
wanted to wake up!

Battersea
Dogs & Cats Home

The next day, Gemma, Mum and Dad
were on their way to Battersea Dogs &
Cats Home. Lorna and Alex had stayed
at home to look after the others. Gemma
felt funny being in the back of the people
carrier all on her own, without Pete and
Matthew pushing and shoving and
Hermione complaining. She stretched out
on the seat and thought about her puppy.

Mum and Dad had explained that they
were going to get him from Battersea
Dogs & Cats Home, a rescue centre where
dogs and cats lived until they found a
new home. They took in all kinds of dogs
from old ones to little puppies, dogs of all
breeds, shapes and sizes. Gemma didn't
really mind what her puppy looked like,
as long as he could woof!

When they got to
Battersea, Gemma
jumped out of the
car. Mum held one
of her hands and
Dad held the
other as they
walked to the
reception.
Gemma
couldn't

remember ever having her parents all to herself before – the puppy was already making her life better and she hadn't even met him yet!

"Now, before we go and see all the dogs we've got to have

an interview," Dad explained, "so they can find out about our home and lifestyle and match us to the best dog. We couldn't have a nervous dog that didn't like people or noise, not in our madhouse!"

Gemma nodded happily. She'd do anything it took to get a puppy of her own. She followed her parents into the reception, where they were met by a nice lady called Mandy, who took them into a

room to ask them some questions. "Wow,
six big brothers and sisters!" she smiled
at Gemma. "Well soon you won't be the
youngest any more, not if
you have a little
puppy to look
after! In fact, I
think I know the
perfect pooch for
you. She's a
dachshund – very
energetic and
she'd like having
lots of people to play
with. Shall we go and see her?"

"Yes *please!*" Gemma said
enthusiastically. Mandy led them into the
kennels, past lots of little rooms with a
dog in each. They all wagged their tails
and barked as Gemma and her parents

walked by. Eventually Mandy stopped in front of a kennel. "This is Petal," she said with a smile. Gemma peered into the kennel and gasped out loud. With her glossy brown coat, shiny wet black nose and huge chocolate eyes, she was absolutely adorable! Petal bounced over to the cage door and jumped up at the wire, her tail wagging like mad. "*Woof!*" she barked, as if she was saying "Hello".

"Hello Petal!" Gemma squealed. "You are SO beautiful!"

"She's certainly full of energy." Mandy laughed as the little pup jumped up and down at the cage door. "Let's take her down to one of our outside paddocks and let her have a run around."

Mandy went to grab a lead, then opened Petal's pen. Petal was leaping around so much that it was hard for her to clip the lead to her collar!

Mandy kept hold of Petal's lead, and Gemma's heart swelled as the excited puppy bounced about at the end of it. Mum and Dad walked behind her holding hands. They looked as happy as she felt!

When they got outside, Petal's tail started wagging even harder. Mandy led them into a decked garden with a little bridge in it. Mandy let Petal off her lead and she shot over the bridge, tail wagging,

and bounded straight into the next
paddock, which was full of fun things for
dogs to play with – a tunnel, a set of
hurdles and even a dog-sized climbing
frame!

"It's like a doggy obstacle course!"
Gemma laughed. "Come on, Petal,
through the tunnel." She crouched down
at one end and peered in. "Pet-al," she
called. "Pet-al!"

All at once Petal came racing through. "*Woof!*" she barked happily as she jumped up at Gemma. She toppled over and Petal clambered on top of her, smothering her face with slobbery licks.

"Oh Gemma!" Mum laughed. But Gemma didn't mind. She was just pleased that Petal was enjoying herself so much!

"Well, I don't think I need to ask this," Dad said, smiling, "but what do you think, Gem, is Petal the puppy you want?"

"Oh yes!" Gemma laughed as Petal licked her nose. "She's absolutely perfect!"

The New Family Member

Gemma fell asleep in the car on the way home, and woke up just as they were pulling into the driveway. She stretched and blinked sleepily. She barely had time to take her seat belt off before the front door burst open and everyone rushed out.

Pete and Matthew pulled open the car door and started asking questions.

"What type of dog is she?" Pete yelled.

"What breed is she?" Matthew asked at the same time.

"She's a dachshund," Gemma said proudly. "Show them the picture, Dad,"

"OK, OK, let's get inside first," Dad grumbled.

When her dad fiddled with his mobile phone Gemma grabbed it impatiently. "You know if I had my own phone . . ." she joked.

"You're getting a puppy, miss!" Dad said, putting his hands on his hips.

"I know! Honestly, I'll never ask for anything else as long as I live," Gemma declared.

"Petal is the most wonderful dog I've ever met. The pictures aren't very good though, because she wouldn't sit still long enough for me to take them!" She passed round the phone and everyone oohed and ahhed at the blurry photos of the little brown dog on top of the climbing frame, leaping up at the camera and wriggling in Gemma's arms.

"She's exactly like I imagined!" Alison breathed.

"We'll help take her for walks," Pete offered. Matthew nodded in agreement.

"I'm so glad I'll get to spend some time with her before I go!"

Lorna added, giving
Gemma a big
squeeze. "When
will we be able
to bring her
home?"

"Mandy said
someone has to
come round and
check that the
house is OK for a
puppy," Gemma
explained. "But it
won't take long. And
she told me that Petal's very energetic
and playful and is going to need lots of
love and attention. So everyone can help
out," she added generously. "With all of
us to love her and play with her, she's
going to be worn out!"

*

Two weeks later, Gemma was waiting
impatiently by the front room window,
looking out into the driveway. Pete and
Matthew rushed in
nosily.

"Is that the
car? We thought
we heard a
noise," they
gasped.

Gemma shook her
head and they went back
upstairs disappointedly. A few hours
earlier, Dad had gone to Battersea Dogs
& Cats Home to pick up Petal. They'd
had a home visit the week before to check
that their house was suitable and safe for
a new puppy, and the Battersea rehomer
had told them that Petal was theirs if

they wanted her – which of course they did!

Everyone was at home waiting impatiently to meet the newest member of the family – now all they needed was for Petal to arrive. *And it was taking ages!* Gemma thought.

"Any sign?" Mum asked, coming in to stand next to Gemma.

"No," Gemma said glumly. Then she caught sight of a flash of blue – Dad's car. "I mean, yes!" she yelled.

"Petal's here! Petal's here, everyone!" she yelled.

There was a waterfall of noise as six pairs of feet galloped to the front door.

"OK, OK, give her space, let her come in," Mum said as the family crowded into the hallway.

"Let me past!" Gemma yelled, elbowing her brothers. "She's *my* puppy!" She jumped up to try and see over Alex's broad back, then dropped to the floor and crawled through the forest of legs, getting to the front door just as it swung open. Dad stood in the doorway, a furry brown bundle in his arms.

Gemma couldn't tear her eyes off the little puppy. Her family gazed at the tiny dog adoringly as Dad came in, shut the door and gave him to Gemma. "Welcome home, Petal!" he smiled. "She's missed you as much as you've missed her," Dad laughed.

Gemma grinned at the warm weight of her puppy in her arms. Petal squirmed about, resting her chin on Gemma's arm as she stared round at everyone. She seemed much tinier than Gemma remembered now that she was actually

in her home! Petal wriggled again, and
Gemma put her carefully down on the
floor. "This is Lorna, and Alison, and
Hermione, and Alex and Pete, and
Matthew and Mum," she introduced her.

"*Woof!*" Petal barked, wagging her tail
as she sniffed at everyone's feet.

Pete and Matthew knelt down either
side of her and started stroking her.
Even Hermione bent down to
touch her silky-soft ears.
"She's so beautiful!"
she told Gemma.
Gemma grinned
proudly.

For a second Gemma felt left out as
her brothers and sisters fussed over Petal.
The pup was enjoying the attention, her
tail was wagging so fast it was a blur. But
then the little puppy jumped up and
started looking around as if she was
searching for something. When she saw
Gemma she gave a happy bark and her
tail started wagging again.

Petal likes everyone, Gemma thought
with a thrill of pride, *but she loves me the
most!*

Petal the Sniffer Dog!

The next few days passed really quickly as Petal settled in. Gemma was so pleased that it was the summer holidays so she could spend all day with her new puppy. The only time they were apart was at night, because Petal wasn't allowed upstairs. Even then, Gemma made sure she saw her all she could. She gave her a cuddle before she went to bed and as soon as she woke up she rushed straight downstairs to feed her. She was the last thing she thought about before she went to sleep and the first thing she remembered when she got up!

Everyone fussed over Petal so much, she was barely ever on her own, but although she seemed to love everyone, her tail always wagged extra hard when she saw Gemma, and when she was downstairs she followed her everywhere. Dad started calling her Petal Shadowpaws because she was always behind Gemma, just like her shadow!

But one morning, just after Gemma had given Petal her breakfast, her friend Rosie phoned and invited her to go swimming.

Gemma didn't know what to do – she loved swimming, but she didn't want to leave Petal. Mum laughed at her worried face when Gemma told her. "Petal will still be here when you get back, Gem," she smiled. "That's the good thing about her being *yours*, forever."

"OK," Gemma decided. "But we'll have extra fun when I get home."

An hour later, Gemma rushed in through the front door, her hair still in damp strands over her shoulders. She'd had fun swimming,

but she was delighted to see her little
puppy again. Petal jumped around her
legs excitedly as if she hadn't seen her for
a week, rather than an hour.

"We took her out for a walk, Gemma,"
Alison told her.

"She nearly tripped me up with her
lead," Hermione grumbled.

"No, you were texting and not looking
where you were going!" Alison giggled.

"Thank you!" Gemma smiled. "We'll
go and play in the garden."

As Petal galloped outside, Gemma tried
to think of something fun they could do.
She thought she'd try and set up a doggy

agility course for her, since she liked the
one at Battersea Dogs & Cats Home so
much.

She was just setting out a line of balls
to make a slalom, with Petal watching
her with interest, when she heard a voice
nearby. "What are you doing?" it
asked. Gemma looked round
in surprise, but there
was no one there.

"Up here!" the voice said. Gemma
looked up and laughed to see her twin
brothers climbing in the tree.

Gemma grinned. "You made me jump!
I'm making an agility
course for Petal."

"We'll help!" Pete
shouted, dropping
to the ground next
to her.

"Yeah," Matthew
added, jumping
down after him. "I
know where there's a
plank of wood we can
use." The boys ran off.

Gemma tried to show Petal the
slalom, running through it and calling
her to follow, but for once Petal wasn't
behind her. She didn't seem at all
interested, she was too busy digging in an
overgrown flowerbed. "Petal!" Gemma
called, but although the little pup's ears

flicked when she heard her name, she
didn't stop digging. For a moment
Gemma felt upset that she was ignoring
her, but then she became curious. Petal
was pawing at the same patch
of earth, putting her nose
right into the dirt and
smelling it
enthusiastically.

"What
have you
found, Petal?"
Gemma asked.

This time
Petal turned at
her name. She
had black earth all
over her little brown face. Even
her ears were spotted with mud, but her
eyes were gleaming and her tongue was

hanging out in a big doggy smile. "*Woof!*" she said proudly, then turned back to the flowerbed.

"You funny pup," Gemma said. "What is it?" She walked over to the flowerbed just as Petal pulled something out of the earth and shook it from side to side, splattering mud everywhere. "Petal!" Gemma squealed, as she dropped the object at her feet.

Gemma bent down to pick it up. It was a watch! She wiped the dirt off the watch with her sleeve and read the inscription, *Happy 18th Birthday!* It was Lorna's watch, the one she'd lost a few weeks ago! She'd had everyone  searching for it after it disappeared. It must have fallen off in the garden and no one had thought to look there!

"Oh! Well done, Petal!" Gemma cried, crouching down to hug the muddy pup. "Lorna's going to be so pleased!"

Gemma rushed inside with Petal running at her feet, barking happily. "Lorna, Lorna!" she yelled as she ran into the kitchen.

Alison, Lorna and Mum looked up

from the kitchen table. "My watch!"
Lorna gasped as she saw it dangling from
Gemma's hand. "Where did you find it?"

"I didn't find it!" Gemma laughed,
"Petal did!"

"Oh, she must have been able to smell
my perfume on the watch strap," Lorna
cried. "Thank you, you clever little puppy.
I'm so glad I helped Gemma get you!"

Mum ruffled Petal's ears. "Well, aren't
you a clever little dog. With
a nose like that you
could have a career
in the police
force!"

"Yes," Gemma
smiled. "Petal the
sniffer dog!"

Fairground Fun

The next day was Saturday, and Gemma was helping Mum and Lorna pack the last of Lorna's things into the car. It was her last day at home before Mum drove her and Alex up to uni the next day, and Gemma was feeling really sad. She lugged a bag into the boot and Petal jumped in after it.

"No Petal, you can't go!" Gemma

laughed. It was a good thing she had her puppy to make her smile.

Just then the twins rushed over, waving a flyer. "Mum, Mum," they yelled. "There's a funfair today in Hollyhill Park!"

"Can we go? Please, please?!" they both shouted.

Mum looked at the flyer and smiled. "Ooh, a funfair." She grinned. "I haven't been to one of those in years. Your dad and I used to go when we were young."

"So can we go? Pleeeeeeease?" Pete pleaded.

"I suppose so," Mum smiled. "We can make it a real family outing!"

"And Petal too?" Gemma asked.

"Well . . ." Mum hesitated. "She is very little, love, she might be a bit too frightened."

"But she's part of the family!" Gemma insisted. "It won't be a family outing without her."

"*Woof!*" Petal agreed.

Mum laughed. "I suppose if we go while it's still light—" she started to say.

"Thanks, Mum!" Gemma cried, leaping up to give her a hug.

"But you have to promise to take really good care of her," Mum said.

"Of course I will! Did you hear that, Petal – we're going to the fair!"

"*Woof! Woof!*" Petal barked, in a way that Gemma knew meant "*Brilliant!*"

After lunch they all walked over to Hollyhill Park together. The park had been completely transformed. Where

there were normally huge fields filled
with people walking their dogs, now there
were rides and stalls everywhere. The air
was filled with the sound of people
shrieking and laughing as they whizzed
round on waltzers and carousels and
dodgems. And in the middle of it all was
a huge Ferris wheel.

Gemma didn't know where to look first
– and Petal didn't know

what to smell! She
trotted excitedly
towards hot-dog
stands and
sniffed at bits of
candy floss that
had been
dropped on the
ground. Gemma
had to keep
making sure she
followed the rest of her
family as they walked around. "There's
too many nice smells for a sniffer dog
here," she joked.

"Look, that toy looks just like Petal!"
Pete yelled, pointing at a large stuffed
dog hanging from one of the stalls.

"You can win it if you knock down all the tin cans," the seller bellowed, "three balls a pound."

"Can we try?" Matthew begged Dad.

"Please!" Pete added.

"Go on then," Dad grinned.

Alex handed some money to the man and gave Pete and Matthew a ball each. "Do you want a go, Gemma?" he offered. Gemma shook her head.

"Girls can't throw anyway," Pete laughed.

"Yes we can," Gemma said indignantly. "I'll show you," she added, taking the ball from Alex and handing him Petal's lead.

"*Woof!*" Petal barked encouragingly.

Pete's ball missed completely. Matthew laughed, but while his made the tins wobble, he didn't knock any over either.

Gemma took a deep breath and threw it as straight as she could. There was a great crash and Pete and Matthew turned to her in amazement. Gemma couldn't believe her eyes – all the tins were on the floor. She'd done it!

"Well done," the stallholder smiled. "Which one do you want?" Gemma pointed at the cuddly sausage dog. The stallholder hooked it down with a long pole and gave it to Gemma. Petal jumped up to sniff at it curiously.

"I'll carry it," Lorna offered. "You've got your hands full with one puppy, you don't need another one to look after!"

"Thanks," Gemma smiled. She decided then and there to give the stuffed dog to Lorna so she could take it to uni. After all, Gemma didn't need a *toy* Petal – she had the real thing!

"What shall we do next?" Alex asked.

"I want to go on the dodgems!" Pete said.

"No, the carousel!" Alison squealed.

Mum and Dad looked at each other.

"OK," Mum said. "Everyone can go and do what they want, we'll meet back here at the coconut shy in an hour.

Don't be late!"

Everyone started talking together at once.

"Let's go on the ghost train!" Matthew suggested.

"Ooh, yes," Gemma giggled. She loved scary rides and movies – as long as she knew it wasn't real, it was fun to be a bit scared!

"OK," Lorna decided, "Alison, Hermione and I will go on the carousel. Why don't you four go on the ghost train?" she said to Alex, Pete, Matthew and Gemma.

"Us five, counting Petal!" Gemma laughed.

"We're going on the
tunnel of love," Dad
laughed, squeezing
Mum and making
kissy noises.

"Gross!" Matthew
groaned.

"That's scarier
than the ghost train!"
Pete joked.

"Come on then, you
lot," Alex said, leading them
towards the ghost train. "Follow me for
the most frightening ride of your life!" he
added with a spooky laugh.

But when they got there the ride didn't
look very scary at all. It was decorated
with funny skeletons and ghosts that
swooped backwards and forwards, but it
was old and a bit crumbly, and one of the

glowing letters that spelled out GHOST
TRAIN was flickering on and off.

Petal let out a low whine as a plastic
ghost fluttered overhead, and Gemma
picked her up and stroked her. "It's only
pretend, Petal," she whispered
comfortingly. The puppy reached up to lick
her nose and then snuggled into her arms.

Pete and Matthew
jumped into an empty
carriage and Alex
pulled the bar down
over their laps.
Gemma was just
about to get in when
suddenly a figure loomed out
of the shadows, making her jump.

The ticket collector stepped into the
light and scowled at Gemma and Petal.
"No dogs allowed," he bellowed.

"She won't be any trouble," Alex argued, "she's only a puppy."

"She'll sit on my lap the whole time," Gemma added.

"No. Dogs. Allowed," the mean man insisted.

"Come on, let's find another ride to go on," Alex sighed. Pete and Matthew gave a chorus of disappointed groans.

"It's OK, you go," Gemma told them, "Petal and I will wait outside."

Alex looked from Gemma to the twins and back again. "Are you sure, Gem?" he asked.

"Yes," Gemma grinned. "Petal is much more fun than some silly old ride anyway!

Besides, I think the ride would have been too scary for her - it's better that we sit this one out."

"OK, we won't be long," Alex told her. "Wait here, all right?"

Gemma nodded. But when Alex jumped into the next carriage and the three of them disappeared into the dark, she looked down at Petal sadly. Being a responsible dog owner was harder than she had thought. Petal looked up and licked her nose. Gemma giggled. It was totally worth it though!

Lost!

Gemma spent a while watching everyone else having fun at the fair. Petal wriggled to be let down, and she put her on the ground, carefully winding the lead around her hand so she didn't run away. Petal pulled impatiently on it, trying to get closer to a nearby food stall.

"Sit," Gemma told her, but the little puppy just looked up at her pleadingly, whining softly.

"OK," Gemma gave in. "They're going to be a while anyway," she said, bending down to stroke her. "So we *could* have a little wander round, as long as we're back before the ride's over."

"*Woof!*" Petal agreed happily as they set off into the fair.

"Where shall we go first, girl?" Gemma laughed.

Petal dragged her over to a candyfloss stall, then a stand where people were hooking ducks out of a big pool, and then she padded over to investigate a helter skelter where people

slid down in sacks and
piled in a heap at the
bottom.

Finally she ran up
to a booth surrounded
by bright lights. "Crazy
Mirrors," Gemma read. Petal pulled her
inside. The little dog rushed right up to
the nearest mirror and barked at her

reflection. Gemma
looked at it and
laughed. In it she
looked tall and thin,
like she'd been
stretched out with a
rolling pin! Petal
was pawing at the
mirror curiously,
trying to get at the
strange dog.

"It's not another puppy," Gemma laughed, "it's just you, you silly old sausage!" She raced Petal over to the next mirror, then the next and the next. Laughing, she stopped at one which made her head look huge and round like a beach ball. Gemma picked Petal up so that her head seemed huge too. She looked so funny with a big head on her tiny body! Gemma wished everyone else was here to see it. She was used to always being with her brothers and sisters, it was strange being on her own.

As she thought that, she gave a gasp. "Oh Petal! I forgot about the others! The ride must be over by now. We have to get back to the ghost train!"

With Petal trotting alongside her, Gemma ran back the way they came. In the mirrors it looked like there were hundreds of Gemmas and Petals running along frantically. Gemma wasn't even sure she was going the right way. Just as she was starting to panic, she saw the exit.

"Phew!" she said, picking up Petal and
hurrying out into the fair.

They rushed out of the hall of mirrors
and stopped dead. Where was the helter
skelter? Where was the hook-a-duck
game? Nothing looked the same and there
were crowds of people pushing past her.

Gemma looked around hopelessly.
She'd been to Hollyhill Park a million
times before, but it all seemed so strange
with the stalls and rides everywhere.
Maybe if she wandered around a bit more
she'd find something she recognized . . .

She started walking in what she thought was the right direction, her feet getting faster and faster to match the way her heart was pounding in her chest. "Is that the stand where I won the toy you?" Gemma asked Petal, rushing up to it. But it wasn't the same place, and the toys weren't friendly-looking dogs like Petal, but toy robots and dolls.

Gemma
set off again,
heading towards the
Ferris wheel. *The ghost
train must be here somewhere*,
she thought desperately. But it was
no good, nothing looked familiar. She
stopped, and Petal looked up at her and
gave a little whine. Gemma picked up the
pup and hugged her as a sob rose to her
throat. "Petal," she sniffed. "I think we're
lost!"

Nose to the Rescue!

Gemma stood in the middle of the
fairground, crying. Petal
licked her tears as they
rolled down her cheeks.
Her mum had always
told her to find a
policeman if she got lost,
but Gemma couldn't see
one anywhere. Alex, Pete

and Matthew would have finished their ride ages ago and be cross with her. Maybe she should try and find her way to the coconut stall where they were meant to meet Mum and the others. Everything would be OK if she could find them there.

"Excuse me," she muttered, as a lady went by with a pram, but the baby was crying and the lady didn't hear her.

"Do you know where the coconut shy is?" she asked a boy about Pete's age.

"Which one? There are loads – this is a funfair, you know!" he smirked.

"*Woof!*" Petal barked at him crossly. The boy

laughed and walked off with his friends.

"If Mum and Dad would let me have a mobile of my own I could just call them now." Gemma crouched down and put her arms round Petal. Then she sighed. "But it's still my fault for wandering off. Oh Petal, what are we going to do? We're lost and we've got no idea how to find our family."

But when Gemma said "family", Petal gave an excited yap and struggled out of her arms. She pulled on her lead as hard as she could, then turned back to look at Gemma as if to say, *"Come on, I know the way."*

Gemma felt a surge of relief. "Family?" she asked. "Do you know what I'm saying? Can you find our family?"

Petal pulled on her lead again.

Gemma smiled through her tears. "Come on then," she grinned, running after the little brown dog. "Find our family, Petal!"

Petal had her nose to the ground as if she was following a scent. *Please don't be leading me to a hot-dog stand!* Gemma thought desperately. Petal pulled her past all the stalls so fast that she had to

concentrate on not tripping up. She kept
her eyes on her feet as she ran along. It
wasn't until she heard someone call her
name that she looked up.

In front of her was the coconut stall,

and in front of that, looking very cross and very relieved all at the same time, were Mum, Dad, Alex, Lorna, Hermione, Alison, Pete and Matthew. Her family!

"Gemma!" Mum called again, running over to wrap her in a tight hug. "Where have you been? We were so worried."

"I told you to stay by the ghost train," Alex said crossly.

"I know, I know, I'm sorry," Gemma sobbed. "I didn't mean to, I just went off for a second and then I couldn't find my way back. Petal saved me – she sniffed the way back to you."

Gemma picked up Petal
and everyone crowded
round to stroke and
pet her.

"You were very
lucky to have
such a clever
pup with
you," Mum
said seriously.
"But you must
never, *ever* go
off on your own
again, especially not
in a crowded place like this –
it's not safe."

"I know we've got a big family, love,"
Dad said, "but that doesn't mean we've
got anyone to spare!"

"I'm really sorry," Gemma said again,

looking round at everyone. Lorna gave
her an extra squeeze.

"I was so scared,"
she told Gemma.
"Are you going to
be OK when I
leave? I'll talk to
you on the phone
all the time, and
I'll come home and
visit lots."

Gemma looked
down at Petal. "I'll be
fine," she smiled at Lorna. "You're still
my big sister, even when you're not at
home. Besides," she laughed, "I've got
Petal to look after me now!"

Lorna laughed too and tickled Petal
between her ears.

"Come on, gang," Mum smiled. "I'll

treat you all to a toffee apple each."

"Wait!" Lorna called as the twins began to race away. "Family hug!" she shouted.

Gemma held Petal close and squeezed in to the group. Petal snuggled into her arms and gave a big puppy yawn. Gemma was suddenly surrounded.  There were legs and arms and bodies everywhere, and she could hardly breathe, but she couldn't help grinning.

"Someone's elbowing me!" Hermione complained.

"Not me!" Pete and Matthew yelled together.

Gemma's grin grew even wider. This
was her big, noisy family, and she was
exactly where she belonged – right in the
middle, with Petal in her arms.

Petal looked up at her and licked her
nose. "*Woof!*" she barked, happily.

Read on for lots more . . .

❧ ❧ ❧ ❧

Battersea Dogs & Cats Home

Battersea Dogs & Cats Home is a charity that aims never to turn away a dog or cat in need of our help. We reunite lost dogs and cats with their owners; when we can't do this, we care for them until new homes can be found for them; and we educate the public about responsible pet ownership. Every year the Home takes in around 10,000 dogs and cats. In addition to the site in southwest London, the Home also has two other centres based at Old Windsor, Berkshire, and Brands Hatch, Kent.

The original site in Holloway

History

The Temporary Home for Lost and Starving Dogs was originally opened in a stable yard in Holloway in 1860 by Mary Tealby after she found a starving puppy in the street. There was no one to look after him, so she took him home and nursed him back to health. She was so worried about the other dogs wandering the streets that she opened the Temporary Home for Lost and Starving Dogs. The Home was established to help to look after them all and find them new owners.

Sadly Mary Tealby died in 1865, aged sixty-four, and little more is known about her, but her good work was continued. In 1871 the Home moved to its present site in Battersea, and was renamed the Dogs' Home Battersea.

Some important dates for the Home:

1883 – Battersea start taking in cats.

1914 – 100 sledge dogs are housed at the Hackbridge site, in preparation for Ernest Shackleton's second Antarctic expedition.

1956 – Queen Elizabeth II becomes patron of the Home.

2004 – Red the Lurcher's night-time antics become world famous when he is caught on camera regularly escaping from his kennel and liberating his canine chums for midnight feasts.

2007 – The BBC broadcast *Animal Rescue Live* from the Home for three weeks from mid-July to early August.

Amy Watson

Amy Watson has been working at Battersea Dogs & Cats Home for eight years and has been the Home's Education Officer for four years. Amy's role means that she organizes all the school visits to the Home for children aged sixteen and under, and regularly visits schools around Battersea's three sites to teach children how to behave and stay safe around dogs and cats, and all about responsible dog and cat ownership. She also regularly features on the Battersea website – www.battersea.org.uk – giving tips and advice on how to train your dog or cat under the "Fun and Learning" section.

On most school visits Amy can take a dog with her, so she is normally accompanied by her beautiful ex-Battersea dog, Hattie. Hattie has been living with Amy for just over a year and really enjoys meeting new children and helping Amy with her work.

The process for re-homing a dog or a cat

When a lost dog or cat arrives, Battersea's Lost Dogs & Cats Line works hard to try to find the animal's owners. If, after seven days, they have not been able to reunite them, the search for a new home can begin.

The Home works hard to find caring, permanent new homes for all the lost and unwanted dogs and cats.

Dogs and cats have their own characters and so staff at the Home will spend time getting to know every dog and cat. This helps decide the type of home the dog or cat needs.

There are three stages of the re-homing process at Battersea Dogs & Cats Home. Battersea's re-homing team wants to find you the perfect pet: sometimes this can take a while, so please be patient while we search for your new friend!

1 Register details

2 Match

3 Leaving with your new pet

Have a look at our website:
http://www.battersea.org.uk/dogs/rehoming/index.html for more details!

"Did you know?" questions about dogs and cats

- Puppies do not open their eyes until they are about two weeks old.

- According to *Guinness World Records*, the smallest living dog is a long-haired Chihuahua called Danka Kordak from Slovakia, who is 13.8cm tall and 18.8cm long.

- Dalmatians, with all those cute black spots, are actually born white.

- The greyhound is the fastest dog on earth. It can reach speeds of up to 45 miles per hour.

- The first living creature sent into space was a female dog named Laika.

- Cats spend 15% of their day grooming themselves and a massive 70% of their day sleeping.

- Cats see six times better in the dark than we do.

- A cat's tail helps it to balance when it is on the move – especially when it is jumping.

- The cat, giraffe and camel are the only animals that walk by moving both their left feet, then both their right feet, when walking.

Dos and Don'ts of looking after dogs and cats

Dogs dos and don'ts

DO

- Be gentle and quiet around dogs at all times – treat them how you would like to be treated.
- Have respect for dogs.

DON'T

- Sneak up on a dog – you could scare them.
- Tease a dog – it's not fair.
- Stare at a dog – dogs can find this scary.
- Disturb a dog who is sleeping or eating.

- Assume a dog wants to play with you. Just like you, sometimes they may want to be left alone.
- Approach a dog who is without an owner as you won't know if the dog is friendly or not.

Cats dos and don'ts

DO
- Be gentle and quiet around cats at all times.
- Have respect for cats.
- Let a cat approach you in their own time.

DON'T
- Never stare at a cat as they can find this intimidating.

- Tease a cat – it's not fair.
- Disturb a sleeping or eating cat – they may not want attention or to play.
- Assume a cat will always want to play. Like you, sometimes they want to be left alone.

Some fun pet-themed puzzles!

What to think about before getting a dog!

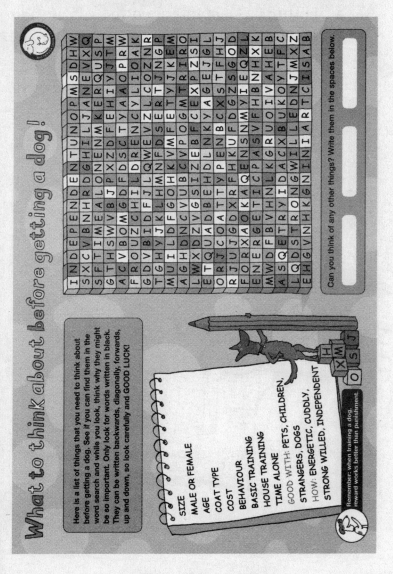

Here is a list of things that you need to think about before getting a dog. See if you can find them in the word search and while you look, think why they might be so important. Only look for words written in black. They can be written backwards, diagonally, forwards, up and down, so look carefully and GOOD LUCK!

SIZE

MALE OR FEMALE

AGE

COST

BEHAVIOUR

BASIC TRAINING

HOUSE TRAINING

TIME ALONE

GOOD WITH: PETS, CHILDREN, STRANGERS, DOGS

HOW: ENERGETIC, CUDDLY, STRONG WILLED, INDEPENDENT

Remember: when training a dog, reward works better than punishment.

Can you think of any other things? Write them in the spaces below.

Tangled Leads and Crazy Maze

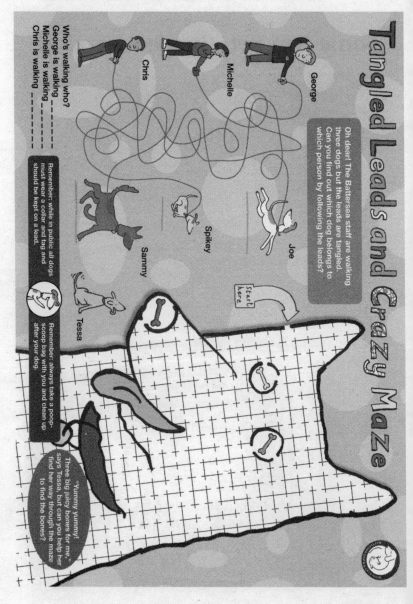

Oh dear! The Battersea staff are walking three dogs but the leads are tangled. Can you find out which dog belongs to which person by following the leads?

George

Michelle

Chris

Spikey

Joe

Sammy

Tessa

Start here

Who's walking who?
George is walking _ _ _ _ _ _ _
Michelle is walking _ _ _ _ _ _ _
Chris is walking _ _ _ _ _ _ _

Remember: while in public all dogs must wear a collar and tag and should be kept on a lead.

Remember: always take a poop-scoop bag with you and clean up after your dog.

"Yummy yummy! Three big juicy bones for me," says Tessa, but can you help her find her way through the maze to find the bones?

Drawing dogs and cats

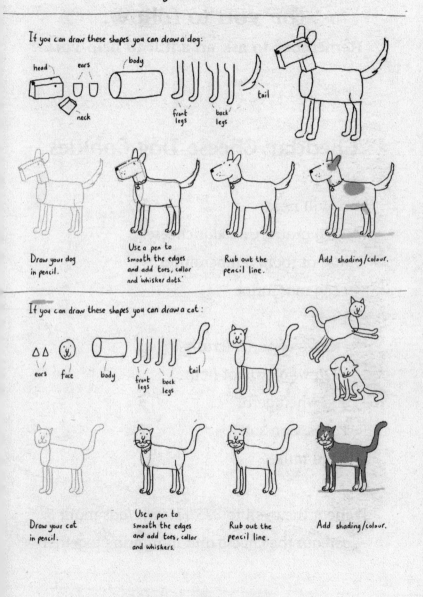

If you can draw these shapes you can draw a dog:

head · ears · body · tail · front legs · back legs · neck

Draw your dog in pencil.

Use a pen to smooth the edges and add toes, collar and 'whisker dots.'

Rub out the pencil line.

Add shading/colour.

If you can draw these shapes you can draw a cat:

ears · face · body · front legs · back legs · tail

Draw your cat in pencil.

Use a pen to smooth the edges and add toes, collar and whiskers.

Rub out the pencil line.

Add shading/colour.

Here is a delicious recipe for you to follow.

Remember to ask an adult to help you.

Cheddar Cheese Dog Cookies

You will need:

227g grated Cheddar cheese

(use at room temperature)

114g margarine

1 egg

1 clove of garlic (crushed)

172g wholewheat flour

30g wheatgerm

1 teaspoon salt

30ml milk

Preheat the oven to 375°F/190°C/gas mark 5.

Cream the cheese and margarine together.

When smooth, add the egg and garlic and mix well. Add the flour, wheatgerm and salt. Mix well until a dough forms. Add the milk and mix again.

Chill the mixture in the fridge for one hour.

Roll the dough onto a floured surface until it is about 4cm thick. Use cookie cutters to cut out shapes.

Bake on an ungreased baking tray for 15–18 minutes.

Cool to room temperature and store in an airtight container in the fridge.

There are lots of fun things on the website, including an online quiz, e-cards, colouring sheets and recipes for making dog and cat treats.

www.battersea.org.uk